MW01110484

The Last Wild Witch
First Printing in Paperback 2014

Published by Mother Tongue Ink
Creators of We'Moon: Gaia Rhythms for Womyn
and other visionary publications for a changing world.
PO Box 1586
Estacada, Oregon 97023
mothertongue@wemoon.ws
www.wemoon.ws
www.lastwildwitch.com
1-877-693-6666 US—Int'l 541-956-6052

Library of Congress control number: 2009923248
Paperback ISBN: 978-1-890931-94-0
Hardcover ISBN: 978-1-890931-59-9

Printed by Sung In America on recycled paper with soy based ink.

Hansol Paper Environmental Benefits Statement:

The Last Wild Witch is printed on Hansol paper using 60% recycled content: 50% pre-consumer waste, 50% post-consumer waste, with Solvent-free Soy and Vegetable Based inks with VOC levels below 1%.

The Last Wild Witch

Written by Starhawk
Illustrated by Lindy Kehoe

Published by Mother Tongue Ink

Once there was a perfect town in a perfect world where there were rules for everything and a right way and a wrong way to do everything and nobody ever broke the rules.

Well, hardly ever.

For on the farthest edge of the perfect town stood the last magic forest, and the forest was wild. The plants and the birds and the animals and the insects and the fish in the streams all lived according to their own natures and didn't follow any rules at all.

In the very heart of the last magic forest lived the last wild Witch. She looked so ordinary that if you met her on the street you might think she was your own grandmother.

All day long she brewed herbs and leaves and berries in her big magic cauldron, making a healing brew that she fed to the birds and the animals and the insects and the fish in the streams whenever they felt a little low.

And all night long she sang enchanting songs and played her drum.

Sometimes, when the wind was from the West, it would carry the fragrance of the magic brew or a few notes of the magic songs into the town. Sometimes, when the children were feeling low or when they left their windows open at night, they'd sniff the brew or hear a snatch of the song, and some of the wildness would get inside them.

In the perfect town, the children always lined up perfectly to walk into their schoolrooms, boys on one side, girls on the other, in proper alphabetical order. They sat perfectly still in their seats and learned their lessons to perfection and nobody ever misbehaved.

Well, hardly ever.

For when the wildness got inside them, they couldn't bear to walk in straight lines. They ran and jumped and danced and turned cartwheels on the perfectly smooth grass. They wouldn't go inside when they were told to. They stayed outside laughing in the sunshine or jumping in the puddles when it rained.

Once in a great while, a few of the children would sneak out at night and run through the forest to visit the last wild Witch. She would wink at them and grin. "Have some soup," she would say, and that is all that she would say.

Once, Janey Green and Johnny Brown stayed out all night long, drinking the Witch's magic brew and dancing with the rabbits and the deer and the birds. And they weren't even tired in the morning.

But their parents were tired, and mad! They'd been very worried when they found their children's empty beds, with pillows stuffed under the blankets to make a hump like somebody sleeping.

"Something must be done!" Johnny's father complained.

"It's all this wildness upsetting things," Janey's mother said. "It's got to be stopped!"

They complained so long and hard that the Mayor finally called a meeting in the Town Hall.

The Mayor talked and the Judge from the High Court talked and all the important grownups spoke at great length, but none of the children were allowed to say a word.

"The wildness comes from the Witch in the woods," the Judge said. "We must stop her."

"How?" asked Johnny's mother.

"The answer is clear," said the Mayor. "We must cut down all the trees, and expose her hiding place."

And that is just what they decided to do.

All the children were very upset. "That's not fair!" Billy Blue protested.

"What about the animals?" Janey Green cried.

But nobody listened to them.

Late that night, when the wind was out of the West, carrying wildness with it, Janey Green, Johnny Brown and Billy Blue snuck out their open windows and ran out into the forest, down the dark paths.

They ran so fast the deer could hardly keep up with them, past the rabbits and the nests of the birds and the streams where fish slept, until they reached the clearing where the Witch was playing her drum, pausing every now and then to stir her cauldron.

“Witch, Witch, the grownups are coming to cut down the forest and chase you away! The birds and the deer and the rabbits and the insects won’t have anywhere to live, and the trees will be dead! You’ve got to do something!” Janey shouted, breathless.

The Witch just smiled. “Have some soup,” she said, and that was all that she said. So the children sipped her magic brew and went home to their beds. They cried themselves to sleep, and then dreamed of the forest being saved.

But the next morning, the grownups of the perfect town gathered up all the axes and hatchets and saws and chainsaws they could find, all kept in perfect repair and razor sharp. They carried them down to the edge of the forest, and the children followed.

The Mayor made a speech. "Today is a bright new dawn! Too long have we allowed wildness and chaos to flourish on the very edge of our town. Today we strike a blow for order!"

All the grownups cheered. The Judge raised an axe, planted her feet firmly apart, and swung at the largest tree.

"THUNK" went the ax as it hit the tree. "EEEE-OWWW!" the tree screamed.
All the grownups were so frightened that they dropped their axes and hatchets and saws and chainsaws and ran back to the town.

They held another meeting.

"This proves that we must put an end to the wildness!" the Judge said.
"But how?" asked Janey's father. "I can't bear that terrible screaming."
"The answer is clear," the Mayor said. "Tomorrow we'll plug our ears with wax and cotton, so we won't hear the trees if they scream!"

Late that night, when the wind was out of the West, carrying wildness with it, Janey Green, Johnny Brown and Billy Blue snuck out their open windows and ran out into the forest, down the dark paths. They ran so fast the deer could hardly keep up with them, past the rabbits and the nests of the birds and the streams where fish slept, until they reached the clearing where the Witch was playing her drum, pausing every now and then to stir her cauldron.

"Witch, Witch, the grownups are coming back tomorrow to cut down the forest and chase you away! They're going to plug their ears so they won't be able to hear the cries of the forest. You've got to do something!" Johnny shouted.

The Witch just smiled. "Have some soup," she said, and that was all that she said. So the children sipped her magic brew and went home to their beds. They cried themselves to sleep and dreamed of the forest being saved.

The next morning the grownups gathered again at the edge of the forest. They carried all the axes and hatchets and saws and chainsaws, and their ears were so plugged with wax and cotton that they couldn't hear a word of the stirring speech the Mayor gave. The children just watched as the Judge took her axe and planted her feet and took a big swing at the largest tree. Only the children could hear the "thunk" the axe made as it bit into the wood, and the pitiful scream of the tree.

"Hurray!" all the people shouted, even though they could not hear each other. But suddenly, from all the trees around, nuts and berries and branches began to rain down. Acorns bounced off the top of the Judge's head. A big branch swatted the Mayor on his backside. All the grownups screamed, and dropped their axes and hatchets and saws and chainsaws and ran back to the town.

They held another meeting.

"This is disgraceful!" the Judge said. "We must end this wildness once and for all!"

"But how?" asked Billy Blue's grandfather.

"The answer is clear," the Mayor said, standing up because he was too sore to sit down. "Tomorrow we must wear hard hats to protect us and padded jackets and elbow and knee pads. And instead of chopping down the trees, we'll burn the forest down."

"But that's dangerous!" Johnny Brown protested. "You might burn the Witch by mistake!"

The Mayor glared at him. "Children should speak only when spoken to," he said, and the meeting ended.

Late that night, when the wind was out of the West, carrying wildness with it, Janey Green, Johnny Brown, Billy Blue and little Sally Violet snuck out their open windows and ran out into the forest, down the dark paths.

They ran so fast the deer could hardly keep up with them, past the rabbits and the nests of the birds and the streams where fish slept, until they reached the clearing where the Witch was playing her drum, pausing every now and then to stir her cauldron.

“Witch, Witch, the grownups are coming, and this time they’re going to wear hard hats and padded jackets and knee and elbow pads, and burn the forest down, and the birds and the deer and the rabbits and the insects and *you*, too! You’ve got to do something!” all the children shouted together, breathless.

The Witch just smiled. “Have some soup,” she said, and that was all that she said. So they sipped her magic brew.

"Why won't you ever say anything to us?" Johnny asked. "Why won't you do something to save yourself?"

The Witch just smiled, and spooned more broth into their bowls. Janey Green took another sip, and then she remembered a dream.

"Maybe we're supposed to do something," she said. "Maybe we're supposed to save the forest!"

"What can we do? We're just kids," asked Billy Blue.

"I have a plan!" Janey said.

The next morning all the grownups gathered at the edge of the forest. They were all bundled up in heavy jackets and knee and elbow pads, so they walked very stiffly, with their arms and legs straight out. On their heads were hard hats of every description, and they carried lighted torches.

The Mayor made another speech, but the grownups' ears were plugged, and they couldn't hear him.

The children weren't listening. They were waiting for the moment when the Judge lifted the biggest torch and held it toward the branches of the nearest tree.

Before she could set the tree on fire, all the children ran into the forest as fast as they could.

“Come back! Come back!” the Judge shouted. “We can’t burn the woods with all you children in it!”

But the children didn’t listen. They ran deep into the heart of the woods, and hid behind the trees with the rabbits and the deer and the birds and the insects.

All the mothers and fathers and grandmothers and grandfathers became quite frantic. They put out their torches and ran into the woods after the children.

The Mayor and the Judge and all the others followed close behind.
"Come back! Come back!" they shouted. But the children stayed hidden.

Soon the grownups began to get very tired of trying to run in their heavy padded jackets. Their knee pads and elbow pads made their legs very stiff. One by one, they began to take the padding off.

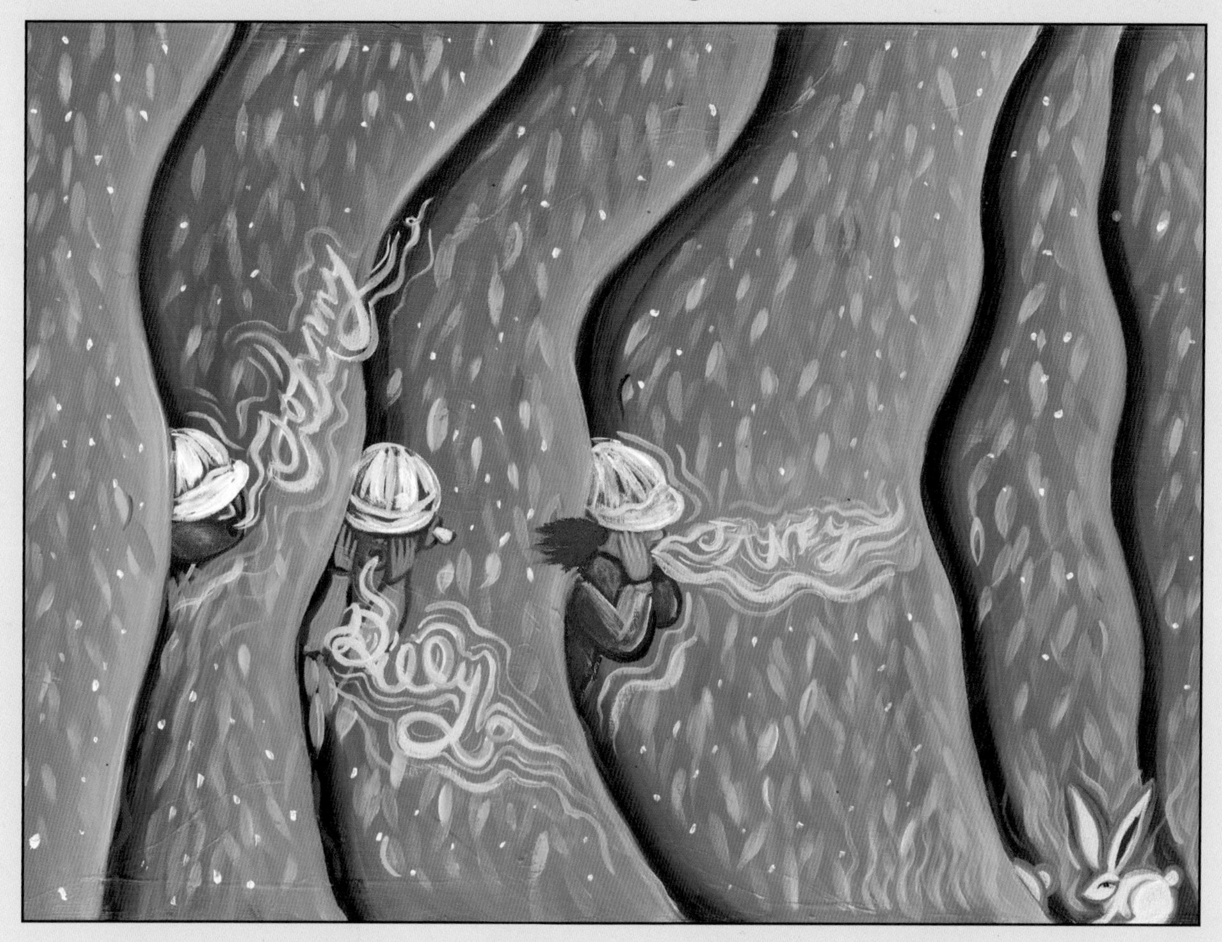

"Janey!" "Johnny!" "Billy!" "Sally!"

The mothers and fathers and grandmothers and grandfathers called, but soon they realized that their ears were plugged and they wouldn't hear the children if they answered. One by one, they began to take the plugs out of their ears.

Without their hard hats and heavy jackets, the people of the perfect town could feel the cool breeze on their arms and the warm sun on their backs. When they took out their earplugs, they could hear the wind in the leaves and the birds singing.

"It's rather pleasant in this forest," Janey's mother said. The Judge glared at her.

“It’s kind of nice by this stream,” Johnny’s father said. “Good fishing, I bet.” The Mayor scowled at him.

But soon even the Mayor and Judge found themselves charmed by the way the leaves danced against the sky. A family of rabbits scurried by the Judge’s ankles, and before she could stop herself, she murmured, “How cute.” A hawk soared above the Mayor’s head. “Magnificent,” he found himself saying.

After a while the grownups began to get very hot and tired. They had walked a long way, and they were hungry and thirsty. Still they could not find their children.

At last they came to the clearing in the center of the forest. There was the Witch, stirring her cauldron and singing her songs. She didn't seem so bad, the grownups thought. Why, she could be anybody's grandmother.

The Witch smiled at them, and winked. "Have some soup," she said.

"Don't mind if I do," the Mayor admitted, and they all sat down and drank some of her magic healing brew, letting just a bit of wildness get inside them.

"Fellow townspeople," the Mayor said, "we have been saved from a grave error by our children. This forest is not so bad. And, Madame," he addressed the Witch, "this soup is delicious!"

"Perhaps we have been wrong," the Judge admitted. "Perhaps we need a little wildness, too."

The children jumped out from their hiding places, and let out a loud cheer. Everybody laughed, and hugged, and then they all stayed up late into the night, dancing with the deer and the birds and the rabbits while the Witch played her drum and sang her songs.

From that day, things changed in the perfect town. The grownups and the children often went to the woods to visit, and sometimes the Witch came to town, especially when someone was sick and needed a taste of magic brew for healing. The children still learned their lessons, but they danced and sang and walked in the woods, and they hardly ever stood in perfectly straight lines. The gardens grew as never before, and the trees bore so much fruit that their branches bent down to the grass, where dandelions and daisies and wildflowers grew.

And sometimes at night, when the wind came out of the west, carrying wildness with it, everybody gathered to dance and sing all night long with the deer and the rabbits and the birds. And they weren't even tired in the morning.

So things were not so perfect in the no-longer perfect town.

But they were better.

The End.

Elizabeth Gorelik

Starhawk is one of the most respected voices in modern earth-based spirituality. She is also well-known as a global justice activist and organizer, whose work and writings have inspired many to action. She is the author or coauthor of ten books, including *The Spiral Dance: A Rebirth of the Ancient Religion of the Great Goddess*, *The Fifth Sacred Thing* and *The Earth Path*. She practices permaculture and teaches courses in regenerative design with Earth Activist Trainings. www.EarthActivistTraining.org. Her website is www.starhawk.org.

Lindy Kehoe is a painter of magical realms and playful characters. Her art echoes the remembrance of the child heart. She lives and loves in Southern Oregon, dreaming of new earth visions, and is a We'Moon contributing artist. She is a fairy tale writer, creating stories that weave myths of all time. To view more of Lindy's work visit: www.lindykehoe.com.

Myshkin

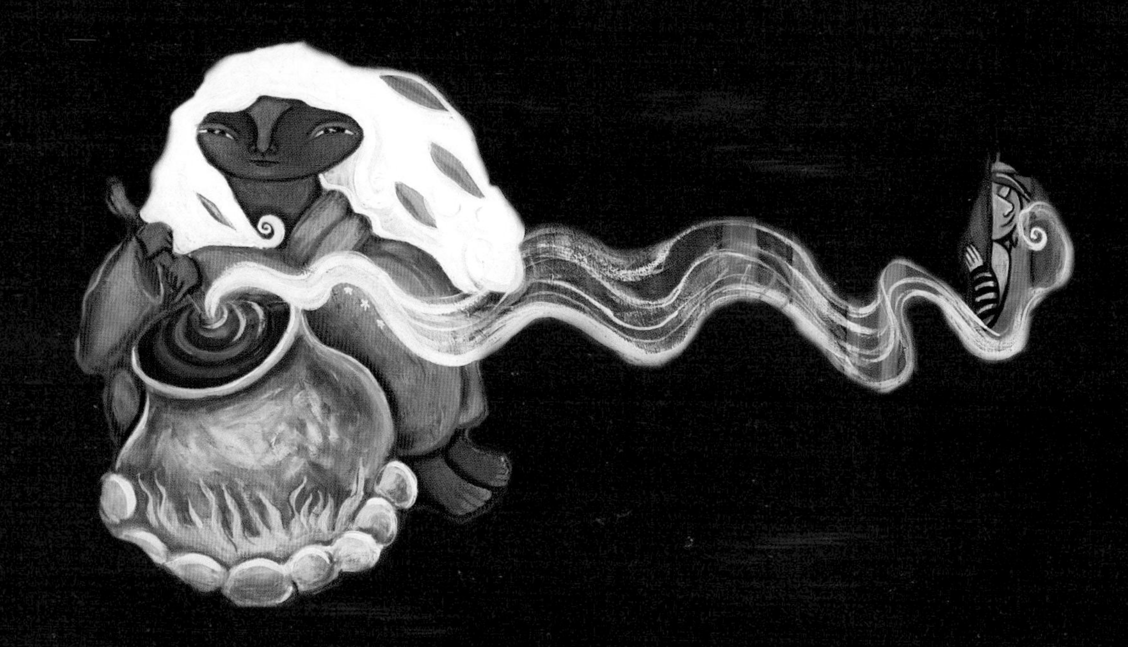

Mother Tongue Ink publications feature creative work by women, celebrating earth-based spirituality and visions for a changing world. Since 1981, MTInk has published We'Moon: Gaia Rhythms for Womyn—the well-known eco-feminist datebook, astrological moon calendar and daily guide to natural cycles—with art and writing from the growing edge of international women's culture. *The Last Wild Witch* is our first children's book.

To order this book, *The Last Wild Witch* poster, or other Mother Tongue Ink products, visit our website or email:
mothertongue@wemoon.ws
www.wemoon.ws
www.lastwildwitch.com